A VERY GRUMPY THANKSGIVING

WOLF VALLEY: A VERY GRUMPY HOLIDAY
BOOK 2

SHAW HART

 Created with Vellum

WANT A FREE BOOK?

You can grab *Sweets* Here.
**Check out my website, www.shawhart.com for
more free books!**

*

We just need to make it through Thanksgiving.

Saffron:

I made a mistake buying this house.

It needs work, more than I am capable of, and I can't afford to hire anyone.

I figure that I'm screwed... until my neighbor offers me a deal.

He'll do the renovations if I pretend to be his girlfriend for Thanksgiving with his family.

Nolan:

I can't do another family holiday where I'm being set up by everyone.

Which is why I made a deal with my new neighbor.

I thought that it would be simple.

We would eat, pretend to be in love with each other, and then go home.

There's just one problem.

The more time that I spend with my curvy fake girl-friend, the more I fall for her.

Now, I need to figure out how to make my fake girl-friend my real one.

ONE

Saffron

I'VE MADE A TERRIBLE MISTAKE.

That realization hits me as I stand on the sagging front porch of the house that I just bought. What was supposed to be my dream home now looks more like a cautionary tale, or maybe like I just got super into haunted houses and Halloween and forgot to take down all of the scary decorations after the holiday passed almost a month ago.

I sigh as I brush a strand of dark red hair away from my face and glance at the peeling paint on the porch columns. If I squint hard enough, I can still see the potential I had glimpsed when I first saw this place, but the reality is harder to ignore, especially when I'm standing in the middle of it.

I've always had this image of myself: shy, quiet, the girl who preferred the company of books over people. And for most of my life, that's exactly who I've been. But when I decided to move to Wolf Valley with my sisters after our parent's deaths, I thought that maybe, just maybe, I could start a new chapter. I'd move to a new town and get a new beginning. I could be whoever I wanted to be. It sounded so simple, so romantic, like something out of the novels that line the shelves of my bookstore, Shelf Indulgence.

When I first saw this house, I fell in love. It wasn't just the way the oak trees framed the front yard or the soft creaking of the porch under my feet. It was the promise of possibility. A house like this—old, charming, with just the right amount of wear and tear—it was begging to be brought back to life. I could picture myself fixing it up, spending weekends painting walls, replacing old fixtures, and maybe even learning how to lay new floors. I'd be a new version of myself here. I'd be handy, capable, and confident. I saw myself growing alongside the house, piece by piece, until it was mine in every way, until the new me felt like the right me.

What I hadn't factored into my daydream was just how much work a house like this would need orjust how terrible I am at home repairs.

Sure, I had a Pinterest board full of DIY projects and a box of tools that I barely knew how to use, but reality set in the moment I stepped inside. The leaky roof, the creaky floors, the wiring that sparked when I flipped certain switches... the house was a project, all right. And I had taken it on without enough money or experience to make it work.

Once again, I've romanticized my life and now I'm stuck dealing with the reality.

It's not that I don't love a challenge. I mean, I've spent the last year opening and running Shelf Indulgence, and if I can handle making a bookstore successful in a small town, I can handle this house. Right?

Only, the bookstore had its own sort of magic. Shelves

filled with stories of love, adventure, mystery. Things always worked out between those pages. This house? Not so much. I spent nearly all of my savings on buying the place, convinced that I could handle the renovations myself. Now that I'm realizing that I can't, I'm screwed cause what I didn't account for was just how expensive and time-consuming it would be to bring this place back to life.

I let out a sigh and pick up the ladder I dragged out of the shed earlier, leaning it against the side of the house. The gutters are clogged with leaves from last fall, another task that should have been dealt with months ago, long before I bought the place. This task feels like one that I can handle and I'm hoping that maybe if I'm successful with it, that my confidence will grow and I'll be able to tackle the next project.

Grabbing my gloves, I climb to the top of the ladder, my hands shaking slightly from both exertion and nerves. As I climb, each rung of the ladder seems more daunting than the last. The wind picks up, making the leaves in the trees rustle softly. I grip the ladder tighter as I reach the top, awkwardly leaning over to scoop out the debris. The ladder wobbles slightly under me, and my heart pounds in my chest. I shouldn't be doing this alone, but I don't exactly have a choice.

My sisters are all busy with their own business and they know about as much about home repair as I do, so they're not any help. I can't afford to hire anyone. My bank account is nearly empty after buying this place. All of my money went into the down payment, leaving me with barely enough to cover basic repairs, let alone hiring professionals to help.

I'm going to need to start saving up so that I can hire a contractor. I've bitten off more than I can chew here. The realization stings, but there's no denying it. I'm in over my head.

Speaking of over my head...

Heights have never been my thing, but I figured I wouldn't be up that high and that maybe it was time to face my fears. How hard could cleaning gutters be, anyway?

The answer comes in the form of the ladder wobbling beneath me. I grip the gutter tighter, my heart racing as I glance down at the ground, which suddenly seems a lot farther away than it did a moment ago. My foot slips, and for a split second, I think I'm going to fall.

Just as I'm about to lose my balance completely, strong hands grab my waist. The sudden contact sends a jolt through me, and I freeze, my breath catching in my throat. For a moment, I wonder if I'm imagining it, but then I hear a low, familiar voice.

"Are you trying to kill yourself, or are you just testing out the house's life insurance policy?"

I look down, and there he is—Nolan, my grumpy, stand-offish neighbor. He's the last person I expected to see today, but here he is, saving me from what would have undoubtedly been a trip to the emergency room. His hands remain firm on my waist as I try to steady myself on the ladder, and for a moment, I can't think of a single coherent thing to say.

From the moment I saw him, I couldn't help but imagine him as one of the heroes from my romance novels—tall, broad-shouldered, with a perpetual frown that made him look both intimidating and fascinating all at once. He's not the kind of man who strikes up casual conversations or waves from across the yard. No, Nolan is more the "stare from a distance and pretend you don't exist" type.

Despite his gruff demeanor, there's something about him that draws me in, something I can't quite put my finger on. Maybe it's the way he always seems so self-assured, so in control. Whatever it is, I've found myself daydreaming about him more than I care to admit.

And now, here he is, saving me like one of those very heroes I've read about a thousand times. Except this is real, and I'm not sure I know how to play the role of the damsel in distress.

His dark eyes meet mine, and I feel a warmth spread through me that has nothing to do with the crisp autumn air. Nolan and I have lived next to each other for a few weeks now, but I've barely exchanged more than a handful of words with him. He moved in around the same time I bought this house, and from day one, he's kept to himself. Distant is putting it mildly. He's the kind of guy who seems to prefer his own company, not one for small talk or neighborly chats. And yet, here he is, holding me steady on the ladder, like some sort of reluctant knight in shining armor.

I've spent more time than I'd like to admit wondering about him. There's something about his brooding demeanor that reminds me of the heroes from my romance novels, the ones who keep their hearts guarded but secretly harbor deep feelings. Sometimes, when I'm lost in my daydreams, I imagine Nolan as the hero, and I'm the heroine he's pining for. Of course, in real life, he's never shown any sign of interest.

Still, there's no denying that he's handsome. Ruggedly so, with dark hair that's always slightly tousled and a jawline that could probably cut through stone. And now, with his hands on me, I can feel the strength in his grip, the solidness of him.

"I—uh—thank you," I stammer, finally finding my voice.

Nolan releases his hold on me and steps back, crossing his arms over his broad chest. He's wearing a flannel shirt rolled up at the sleeves, exposing muscular forearms that only add to his whole grumpy lumberjack vibe. His expression is as unreadable as ever, but there's a flicker of something in his eyes. Concern, maybe? Or annoyance?

"You shouldn't be doing this alone," he says, his tone gruff.

I blink, taken aback. I've lived next to him for months, and this is the longest conversation we've ever had.

"It's just the gutters," I reply, trying to brush off the near-disaster.

"Yeah, and you almost fell off the roof."

"I wasn't on the roof!" I protest, though I know he's right. If he hadn't shown up, I probably would've been on my way to the hospital by now.

Nolan doesn't seem convinced.

"You shouldn't be up there alone," he says again, his tone gruff, as if he was scolding me.

"I, um... I'm fine," I manage, though the slight tremble in my voice probably gives me away. I wasn't fine. I was flustered, embarrassed, and way too aware of how close he was standing.

He folds his arms over his chest, his biceps straining against the fabric of his worn-out T-shirt. "Doesn't look like you've got this under control."

I bristled a little at that. Sure, I wasn't exactly *succeeding*, but I was trying. And maybe it wasn't going perfectly, but that didn't mean I was helpless.

"I've been handling it," I say, a bit more defensive than I intended.

His eyes flicker to the tools scattered around the yard and front porch, then back to me. "Uh-huh."

I exhale sharply and cross my arms, trying to regain some sense of dignity. "I'm just... I'm learning as I go."

His brow lifts, skepticism clear in his expression, but he doesn't argue. Instead, he shifts his weight and glances up at the roof. "That's dangerous. You should hire someone."

"I can't," I blurt, then immediately regret it. The last thing I wanted was to admit to him, of all people, that I was in way over my head. But there it was, out in the open.

His gaze softens slightly, though his expression remains unreadable. "You can't, or you won't?"

I sigh, feeling the weight of my situation settles back onto my shoulders. "I... I can't afford it," I admit quietly. "I spent everything on buying the house. I don't have anything left to hire help."

Nolan is silent for a moment, his eyes scanning my face as if he is weighing his next words carefully. When he finally speaks, his voice is a little less gruff, almost... concerned. "You can't do this all on your own, Saffron."

I blink, surprised he even remembers my name. We've had exactly two conversations before this, both of them awkward, and he'd always seemed more interested in keeping to himself than in getting to know me.

"I'll figure it out," I mumble, not meeting his gaze. I had to. I don't have a choice.

But the truth is, I was starting to realize I've bitten off more than I can chew. The house needs way more work than I'd anticipated, and I was only one person with very little DIY experience. The roof alone is a nightmare, not to mention the plumbing, the electrical issues, and the peeling paint. I'm overwhelmed, and no amount of internet tutorials is going to fix that.

Nolan shifts again, and I can feel his eyes on me, but I don't dare look up. It's bad enough that I'd nearly fallen off the roof in front of him. I don't need him seeing the cracks in my carefully built facade too.

"If you need help," he says after a long pause, "you should ask."

I blink, surprised by the offer. He doesn't strike me as the helpful type, at least not with how standoffish he's been since moving in. And yet, here he is, catching me before I fall and offering... what, exactly?

For a moment, neither of us says anything. The wind rustles the leaves in the trees, and I can hear the faint hum of traffic from the road in the distance. I expect Nolan to walk away, to go back to whatever it is he does all day in his house. But instead, he surprises me.

"Thanks, but I'm okay," I say quickly, even though I know it's a lie.

He clears his throat, giving me a long, measured look before nodding once. "Suit yourself."

With that, he turns and walks back to his side of the yard, leaving me standing there, heart pounding, wondering if I've just made a huge mistake.

I watch him go, biting my lip as I imagine what it would be like if he were the hero in one of my books. The brooding, handsome neighbor, swooping in to save the day, and me—the damsel in distress, swept off her feet. But this isn't a story. It's real life. And in real life, grumpy neighbors don't just offer to fix your roof and sweep you off your feet.

Right?

I sigh and look up at the house again, trying to let go of my romantic daydreams about my grumpy neighbor and get back to work.

TWO

Nolan

SHE FELT SO damn perfect in my arms.

That's the first thought that hit me as I caught her; her body pressed up against mine for just a few seconds longer than it should have been. I was almost afraid to let go. Afraid that the moment I do, she willdisappear like some daydream I've had a thousand times before, but no, Saffron is very real.

Warm. Soft.

Perfect.

I grunt, setting her down as gently as I can, though I try not to linger, pulling my hands away like her skin might burn me. Her cheeks flush pink, and she mumbles a thank you, avoiding my gaze like I'm some sort of grumpy ogre instead of just a man who doesn't know how the hell to talk to her.

That's the problem, though, isn't it? I've never known how to talk to women, and Saffron? She's in a whole different league. A class of her own. Someone like me has no business even standing next to someone like her, let alone catching her off a ladder, like some kind of hero.

Not that she's noticed me much. I've been in Wolf Valley for six months, but to her, I've just been the grumpy neighbor next door. Hell, she hardly even looked at me when she first moved in. She had her nose buried in one of those books she's always reading. It was probably some romance where the guy knew exactly what to say, what to do, and how to win the girl.

Not like me.

I moved to Wolf Valley for the quiet. A fresh start. I needed to get away from... well, from everything. The noise, the pressure. Life back home had felt too loud, too crowded. I figured a small town in the middle of nowhere would suit me just fine. I didn't need much, just some space, some solitude. But then Saffron bought the house next door.

I didn't know what to think when I first saw her, moving boxes into that rundown house like it was some grand palace instead of the money pit it is. She was smiling, bright-eyed, and full of hope, while I stood there watching, arms crossed like the brooding idiot I am. And when I found out she'd just opened a bookstore in town a few months prior? Well, that about did me in.

Saffron Baker isn't built for this place. Not for that house, not for the mess she's gotten herself into. I could see it clear as day. She's delicate, fragile, like some kind of dream you're scared to touch because you might ruin it. And me? I'm a bull in a China shop, always have been. At close to six and a half feet tall, I've always towered over everyone and felt so out of place no matter where I was.

She thanks me again, her voice soft, and I grunt, nodding as I look away. "You should be more careful," I manage, though it comes out harsher than I intend. She doesn't need a lecture, but my nerves are shot, and I can't get my thoughts straight with her standing so close. She stares up at me, biting her lip, and the blush on her cheeks deepens.

"What?" I ask, trying to sound normal, but failing miserably.

Her eyes widen, and she looks away quickly, flustered. "Nothing," she stutters, and I can tell she's lying. She's thinking something, but I'm not good at reading people, especially not women like Saffron. I want to ask her what's on her mind, but before I can, my phone rings, jarring me out of the moment.

I glance at the screen and groan inwardly. It's my mom. Of course, it's my mom.

"Uh, I've got to take this," I say, excusing myself awkwardly, grateful for the distraction but also regretting it immediately. Saffron gives me a small nod, her eyes dropping back to the tools scattered around the yard, and I turn away, answering the call as I walk back to my side of the fence.

"Hey, Ma."

"Nolan! About time you answered. I've been trying to reach you all week," she says, her voice full of that motherly concern I know all too well.

"Yeah, I've been busy," I lie, glancing back toward Saffron, who's already fiddling with something near the ladder, trying to clean up after her little roofing adventure.

"Well, I'm glad I caught you. I wanted to ask you if you were planning on coming home for Thanksgiving?"

I stiffen. Thanksgiving. Right. I'd been trying to avoid this conversation. My mom had been on a kick lately, always trying to set me up with someone from her church or one of her friends' daughters. It was getting exhausting making up excuses to avoid them.

"I don't know, Ma. I might be... busy," I say, not committing to anything. I can practically hear her narrowing her eyes at me through the phone.

"Busy? On Thanksgiving?"

I run a hand through my hair, glancing back at Saffron again. She's messing with a screwdriver now, completely oblivious to the fact that my stomach is in knots. "Yeah, actually. I might be spending it with my girlfriend," I blurt out without thinking. The moment the words leave my mouth, I want to smack myself.

Girlfriend? Really, Nolan?

My mom goes silent on the other end of the line, and I can already tell I've just opened a can of worms I won't be able to close.

"Girlfriend?" she asks, her voice pitched with excitement. "Why didn't you say anything earlier? Who is she?"

I glance back at Saffron again, and before I can stop myself, I answer, "Saffron."

"Saffron," my mom repeats, like she's tasting the name, savoring it. "Oh, I like that. Pretty name. So, when do we get to meet her?"

I inwardly curse myself again. This is getting out of hand. "I don't know, Ma. We're... still figuring things out," I hedge, trying to dig myself out of the hole I've just dug.

"Well, bring her with you! You can come before Thanksgiving or even after if that works better for you two. You know your father and I don't mind adjusting the schedule. Just let me know when you're coming."

I grimace, trying to keep my voice neutral. "Yeah, I'll... I'll talk to her about it."

"Good! I can't wait. You know, I've been waiting for you

to settle down, Nolan. You're not getting any younger, and I'd love to see you with someone special."

I want to groan, but I keep my mouth shut. "Right. Well, I've got to go, Ma. I'll talk to you later."

She chirps something cheerful in response before hanging up, and I'm left standing there, staring at my phone like it's personally betrayed me.

Great. Now I'm screwed.

I glance back toward Saffron, who's still cleaning up, completely unaware of the mess I've just created for both of us. How the hell am I supposed to explain to her that I just told my mom we're dating? She'll probably laugh in my face. Or worse, she'll think I'm a complete idiot.

I run a hand down my face, feeling the weight of my own stupidity settle over me like a heavy blanket. I've always been a man of few words, someone who prefers to keep things simple. But this? This is anything but simple.

Now, I've got to figure out how to convince Saffron to pretend to be my girlfriend for Thanksgiving.

Perfect. Just perfect.

THREE

Saffron

I LOVE mornings in the bookstore, the quiet before the rush of regulars who come in for their latest reads or to sip on coffee while browsing the shelves. Shelf Indulgence had become my little corner of the world, a safe space where I could escape into books and stories—where everything made sense.

But today, I can't seem to focus. My mind keeps drifting back to yesterday, to the feel of Nolan's hands on my waist, steadying me when I'd nearly fallen off the roof. His touch had been firm but surprisingly gentle. And for just a moment, as he caught me, I'd let myself imagine that I was the heroine in one of my novels, and Nolan was the brooding hero coming to my rescue.

But that's not real life, I remind myself. Nolan isn't some fictional knight in shining armor. He's just my grumpy neighbor, a man who barely speaks to me, let alone sees me the way I secretly wished he would.

I sigh, running my fingers along the spine of a book I was supposed to be shelving. The truth was, I had a stupid crush on him. I'd noticed him the moment he moved in next door, tall and brooding, with that jawline that looked like it belonged on the cover of one of my romance novels. But he hadn't noticed me—not really. Not until yesterday, anyway.

The bell above the door jingles, and I glance up, expecting to see one of my regulars, but when my eyes land on Nolan standing in the doorway, all thoughts of shelving books fly right out of my head.

"Nolan?" I blurt, my heart skipping a beat.

He never comes into the bookstore. In fact, I'd never seen him set foot in here before. I'd always figured he wasn't much of a reader.

He doesn't say anything at first, just stands there, looking around the store like he's searching for something. Or someone.

"Are you... looking for anything in particular?" I ask, my voice coming out a little higher than usual. I tried to steady my nerves, but it was hard when he was standing there, all serious and intense.

His gaze flicks to mine, and for a moment, I could have sworn the air between us shifted. "Yeah," he says slowly, his voice low and rough. "I'm looking for you."

My heart thuds in my chest.

Me? He couldn't possibly mean that the way it sounded.

It feels like something straight out of a romance novel, and I swallow hard, trying to rein in the flood of feelings threatening to overwhelm me.

"What... what do you mean?" I manage, my voice is a little shaky as I force myself to meet his eyes.

Nolan steps further into the store, his presence

suddenly filling the space in a way that makes it hard to breathe.

"I need to talk to you about something," he says, his tone serious, and I can tell by the look on his face that this isn't just a casual visit.

"Okay," I say slowly, setting down the book I'd been holding. "What's going on?"

He runs a hand through his dark hair, glancing toward the front door to make sure no one else is around before turning back to me. "I... I told my family that we're dating."

I blink, certain I haven't heard him right. "What? You what?"

"I told my mom we were dating," he repeats, rubbing the back of his neck, looking slightly uncomfortable. "It just... slipped out."

My heart sinks. Oh. So that was why he was here. This wasn't some romantic declaration. This was a mess.

"How does that just...slip out? Why would you do that?" I ask, feeling a knot of disappointment form in my chest.

I try to ignore that sinking feeling as I study him.

Nolan sighs, stepping closer to me, his eyes meeting mine. "Because my mom's been trying to set me up with half the town, and I just... panicked, okay? I told her I was seeing someone, and when she asked me who, the first name that popped into my head was yours."

I stare at him, trying to process what he was saying. "So... you lied."

"Yeah," he admits. "And now she expects me to bring you to Thanksgiving."

The room feels suddenly smaller like the walls are closing in.

Thanksgiving with Nolan's family? Pretending to be his girlfriend?

I open my mouth to say something, but no words came out.

"I know it's a lot," Nolan says quickly, his tone softer now. "But I'm here to make you a deal."

"A deal?" I echo, my mind racing.

He nods, his expression serious. "I've seen you trying to fix up that house, Saffron. You're going to hurt yourself—or worse—if you keep going at it alone."

I bristle a little, even though he isn't wrong. "I'm managing," I mumble, though we both know I'm not.

Nolan crosses his arms, his gaze steady. "Let me help. I'll fix the house, get it into shape so you don't kill yourself trying to do it. In exchange, you come to Thanksgiving with me. Just pretend to be my girlfriend for one day, and we'll call it even."

I stare at him, my mind spinning. This feels like something straight out of one of my romance books—a grumpy, brooding hero making a deal with the heroine, all in the name of convenience. But this wasn't a story. This was real life.

"Why me?" I ask quietly, my heart pounding. "You could have told your mom you were dating anyone. Why pick me?"

Nolan hesitates, his jaw tightening for a moment before he speaks. "Because... you're the only person I could think of. You're my neighbor. We see each other all the time. It just made sense."

I don't know what to say. Part of me wants to turn him down, to tell him this was ridiculous. But another part of me —an embarrassingly large part,is tempted. I need help with the house. That much was obvious. And spending more time with Nolan? I can't deny that the thought makes my heart flutter.

But can I really do this? Can I pretend to be his girlfriend and not let my feelings get in the way? I already have a crush on him, and the last thing I need is to fall for him even more. I'm not sure my heart could take it.

"I don't know," I say, biting my lip as I look away.

"I'm not asking for much, Saffron," Nolan says, his voice gentle. "Just one day. One Thanksgiving. In exchange, I'll fix up your house, and you won't have to worry about getting hurt trying to do it yourself."

It was tempting. So tempting. And the truth was, I needed help. The house was too much for me to handle alone, and I couldn't afford to hire anyone. Nolan's offer was a lifeline.

But what about my heart?

I swallow hard, trying to push down the rush of emotions swirling inside me. "Okay," I say finally, my voice soft. "It's a deal."

Nolan's blue eyes met mine, and for just a moment, I think I see something flicker in his expression—something deeper, something real. But then it's gone, replaced by the same stoic mask he always wears.

"Good," he says, nodding once. "I'll come by tomorrow and take a look at the house."

I nod, feeling a strange mix of anticipation and dread settle over me. "Okay."

As Nolan turns to leave, I watch him go, my heart still racing. This isn't a romance novel, I remind myself. This is just a deal—a simple arrangement.

Now, I just have to make sure I don't fall in love with him even more.

FOUR

Nolan

SHE SAID YES.

Even now, I still can't believe that she agreed to my crazy plan.

She must really need help with the house, I think as I head over to her place, my toolbox in one hand and water bottle in the other. I gingerly walk up the creaky front porch steps and knock on the door. Saffron's car is still parked out front, so I know that she's home.

She opens the door a minute later and I open my mouth, but no words come out.

I've been lying to myself all morning, telling myself that this arrangement is just mutually beneficial, that it's just a business deal, a transaction, but that's not true, and as I stare at Saffron, I can't deny the truth any longer.

I want her. I want her more than anything and I'm hoping that maybe she'll start to develop feelings for me too over the next few days. Maybe if I'm a good fake boyfriend, she'll want to make this thing real.

"Morning, I was just about to head out to work, so perfect timing," she says softly, opening the door wider and ushering me in.

I follow her into the old, rundown kitchen and set my things down on the counter as I look around. The house really does need a lot of work, and I start to make a mental list as I take it in. My eyebrows raise when I see the hammer sticking out of the wall in the kitchen, and she blushes.

"I, uh, I tried to do some repairs myself. It didn't exactly go as planned," she mumbles.

I bite back a smile and nod as I turn to survey the rest of the kitchen.

"Are you sure that you can handle all of this?" Saffron asks me quietly, looking skeptical, and I nod.

"Yeah."

She doesn't look convinced, so I elaborate.

"My dad owns a construction company, and I grew up working for him. I can handle all of this," I promise her.

She nods, looking relieved, and then passes me a paper. I look at it and see that she's made a list of things that need to be fixed.

"I don't have a ton of supplies here right now, but if you give me a list of what you need, I can go to the hardware store or lumber yard and pick it up today."

"Okay. I'll do a walk-through and see what I can start on now and what we'll need."

She nods, and we stand there for a moment, staring at each other. Saffron's face starts to turn pink and I would give everything that I have to know what she's thinking about right now.

Before I can ask her, though, she blinks and turns away from me.

"I should get to work, but you have my number. Let me know if you need anything."

I nod, and she nods back and then heads for the door. I watch her leave and then turn back to her place and take a deep breath. Her sweet strawberry scent lingers here. I breathe deeply, enjoying myself as I start to walk through the house room by room.

I make a list as I go, writing down tasks and supplies needed for it. I have enough materials to get started on some of the smaller tasks, so I spend my morning removing most of the small half-bath downstairs. The toilet and vanity are all outdated and need to be replaced, but we need to fix the floor boards first.

"Whoa, you got quite a bit done, huh?" Saffron asks as she comes up behind me in the bathroom.

She seems impressed as she studies the now demolished bathroom.

"A bit. You'll need to pick out new furniture and all that, but I need to replace some of the flooring first, so you have some time."

She nods, taking a tentative step closer as she looks around the small space.

"I should paint too," she murmurs, and I nod.

"I can do that."

"*I* can do that. You're already doing so much for me."

"I don't mind. It's part of the deal," I remind her, and she nods slowly.

She seems almost disappointed at the reminder of our deal and I wonder if that's a good sign or not.

"I brought lunch," she says, holding up the brown paper bag in her hand.

"You didn't have to do that."

"I wanted to," she says simply, and I smile as I follow her into the kitchen.

"Do you always come home for lunch?" I ask her as she starts to take the sandwiches out of the bag.

"No, not really. I have Ginger watching the store for me right now though. I wanted to see if you had that list of supplies for me, and I was going to run to the hardware store and wherever else."

"Yep."

I pass her the list I made earlier, and her eyebrows raise when she sees how long it is. She seems shocked at the length, and then I see it—worry. I know that she said she couldn't afford to hire someone, and I wonder briefly about her finances.

"I can call around and use some of my family's contacts to get you some good deals. If we buy it in bulk for all of the projects, then that will be cheaper, too."

She nods, looking a little relieved, and I feel like a hero for helping to lighten her load.

"Why aren't you working for your dad and his company?" she asks me as she passes me a sandwich.

"It just wasn't for me. I wanted to make my own way, so I left when I was eighteen and joined the military. The Air Force. Ironically, I was put into structures."

She blinks, looking confused, and I rush to clarify.

"Structures is a career field. They do repairs on the buildings and build stuff."

"So, you left and ended up doing the same thing," she says, and I nod.

"Yeah, and for less money."

"Do you regret it?" she asks, and I shake my head.

"No, it got me out of my small town. I got to see the world, make some friends, and spread my wings a bit."

"And then you got out," she guesses, and I nod.

"Yeah, I was deployed, and one night, there was an air strike. A bomb ended up landing on my building, and I was hurt pretty badly. I was airlifted to the base in Germany, and then a few weeks later, I was discharged and sent back home."

"And you came to Wolf Valley?"

"It seemed like a good place to settle down," I tell her, and she nods.

"What about you? What brought you to this small town?"

"My sisters," she says with a small smile. "My parents passed away, and it just got to be too hard to stay in our childhood home with all of the memories. Olive wanted a fresh start and it seemed like a good idea, so we all followed her here."

"Olive is the oldest?"

"Yeah, then Maple, then me, and then Ginger."

"You guys are close."

"Yeah, they're all my best friends. Do you have siblings?"

I nod, and she takes a big bite of her sandwich.

"Two younger sisters and a younger brother."

"Do they all look up to you?" she asks.

"I doubt it."

I take a bite of food, and she frowns.

"You're not close to them?"

"Not especially. I talk to them like once a month, see them on holidays, but that's it. They all are married with kids and are busy."

She nods, and we eat in silence for a minute.

"Do you want that?" she asks quietly, and I swallow.

"Want what?"

"A wife and kids. A real one," she stresses, and I smile slightly.

"Sure. With the right person."

Our eyes lock, and we stare at each other for a beat.

"What about you?" I ask her, and she looks away, gathering up the wrapper from her sandwich and the napkins.

"Yeah, I want that," she whispers.

I can hear the longing in her voice, and I vow right then and there to give her anything that she needs. I'll be whatever she needs, whatever she wants. I just need her to be mine.

"Let's go get your supplies," I say, my voice rough, and she nods.

I follow her to my truck, and a plan starts to form in my mind for making Saffron more than just my fake girlfriend.

FIVE

Saffron

FOR THE FIRST time in forever, I'm actually excited to go home for the day, and I know that it's all because Nolan will be there waiting for me. He got so much done yesterday, and surprisingly, shopping for supplies with him was fun. The total was a lot less than I was expecting, and I know that I have him to thank for that, too.

We left the lumberyard yesterday with a whole truckload of wood, and I was able to order a bunch of the bathroom fixtures, too. They won't be in for a few weeks, but Nolan says that's okay since it will take him time to fix the floor and paint.

It's so nice to see my vision of the house finally starting to come to life. It's also a huge relief to not have to worry about that project anymore. I trust Nolan, and I know that my house is in good hands with him.

"I got pizza!" I announce as I step inside my place.

Nolan sticks his head out of the bathroom, wiping sweat from his forehead with the back of his gloved hand.

"Pepperoni?" he asks, and I smile.

"Of course."

I had asked him about his favorite foods yesterday when we were driving around together. I figure that the least I can do is feed him. Our deal isn't really fair. He and I both have to be able to see that it's heavily in my favor. I mean, he's fixing up my whole house, and I'm going to one family holiday meal with him in return.

Why does he even need a fake girlfriend? I mean, Nolan is so handsome. I'm sure that he could convince anyone to go out with him. So, why me?

"You don't have to keep feeding me," he tells me as he heads into the kitchen and starts to clean up.

I watch the muscles in his back flex as he leans over the sink and washes his hands.

"I don't mind. I mean, we both have to eat. It will be nice to cook in the kitchen here once that's finished," I say, looking around the space.

"I'll work on that next."

"Oh, I didn't... I wasn't saying that to rush you or anything," I start, and he shakes his head.

"No, it will work out since the cabinets will be in before the bathroom stuff."

I nod and grab some paper plates, handing one to him.

"How was work?" he asks as we each grab a slice.

"It was good. Busy. We started up some book clubs, and they all came in today to pick out their next book of the month."

"That's a good idea."

"Thanks. It's helped with business. It was Ginger's idea, actually. She's amazing with all this marketing stuff."

"Does she own part of the bookstore?" he asks me, and I shake my head.

"Nope, it's just mine. She helps us all out with our shops. She's still trying to figure out what she wants to do with her life."

"How did you land on a bookstore?" he asks as he takes a big bite of his slice.

"I've always loved books. Out of all of us, I was the shyest. I was the quiet, nerdy sister who always had her face buried in a book, so opening my own bookstore was kind of a no-brainer."

He smiles slightly, and I grab a slice and add it to my plate.

"What about you? What will you do now that you're out of the military?"

"Well, I have some time to figure it out. I don't need much, and I get checks now that I'm medically discharged."

"You haven't been getting bored? Just staying home all of the time?" I ask him curiously, and he shrugs.

"A bit. Doing this has been helping," he says with a small smile, and I laugh.

"Well, I'm happy to help. If you ever feel bored after all of this, let me know and I'm sure that I could find something else for you to do."

I don't mean for that to come out so sexual, but it does. My cheeks flame and I know that they must be as red as my hair as I stare at Nolan. He's staring at me, his pizza slice halfway to his mouth. I can't tell if I'm waiting for him to say something or if I would rather that the ground opened up and swallowed me whole.

"I—" I start, but I'm saved by my phone ringing. "Oh, thank god," I mumble as I scramble to answer it. "Sorry, I should take this," I tell him, and he nods.

"Hello?" I answer as I head out to the front porch.

"Hi, I'm with Cellular Live, and I was calling to see if you would be interested in switching over your phone—"

I hang up and groan as I scrub my hands down my still-hot face. *I need to get it together,* I think as I head back inside. *Remember that this is just fake to him.*

"I was thinking, we should get our story straight," I tell him as I head back into the kitchen.

"Story?"

"Yeah, you know? Like what we're going to tell your family."

"Tell them about what?" he asks with a frown.

"Us? I'm sure that they'll have questions. My sisters would want to know where we met, what our first date was, who asked who out, that sort of thing."

"Oh. Right."

"What have you already told them?" I ask as I finish off my slice.

"Just that you're new to town too and that you're my neighbor."

"Okay, that's good. We can just stick as close to the truth as possible then so that it's easier to remember."

"Okay."

"We'll say that we met when I moved in, that you asked me out, and that our first date was at the Italian place in town. Sound good?"

"Sure."

My phone buzzes, and I look at the screen to see Ginger's name.

"I have to get back to the bookstore," I tell him. "I'll see you later."

He nods, and I stuff the pizza box in the fridge before I head back to my car and make the short drive into town.

Ginger was covering for me at the shop again today and I smile at her as I walk in and see her behind the counter.

"Hey, thanks for watching things here."

"No problem," she says with a wide smile. "How's your man?"

I roll my eyes at her question. My sisters know all about Nolan and me. I told them as soon as he asked me because I wanted to know if I was making a mistake. They assured me that it was a good idea, but now I'm having doubts.

The way that we talk, the way that he is around me, it all just feels so natural. With such a big family, it's easy to disappear, but Nolan makes me feel seen, truly seen, for the first time in forever. It's easy for me to forget that this is all fake, just some deal.

And that's dangerous.

"He's good. The bathroom and stuff is coming along really well."

"And? Has he declared his undying love for you yet?" she asks, and I snort.

"Nope."

She sighs, and I smile as I join her behind the counter.

"This isn't a romance book," I say, trying to remind both of us of that fact.

"I've seen the way that he looks at you. Plus, there has to be a reason why he asked you and not someone else."

"I think that he just lied and said he was dating me because I was there when his mom called. I don't think he sees me like that," I tell her.

"Hmm," she says as she twirls an envelope in her fingers.

"What's that?" I ask, desperate to change the subject.

"A note."

"From who?"

"I don't know."

I frown at her, and she smiles sheepishly.

"It's from a secret admirer," she admits, and I grin at her.

"What!? Why didn't you tell me when I first came in? How long has this been going on? Is that the first message? What does it say?" I ask her, and she ducks her head, a pink blush staining her cheeks.

"I've gotten a few before, but they've been more frequent for the last two months or so."

"Why didn't you tell us?"

"Honestly, I thought that it was a joke at first, or maybe given to the wrong person."

She passes me the note and I laugh.

"Ginger, it's addressed to you. How could it be to the wrong person?"

"I don't know! I just... didn't believe that it was for me."

I don't ask her why. I have a feeling that if it had been me, I wouldn't have believed it either. It seems Ginger and I both have some self-esteem issues that we need to work on.

"What are you going to do now that you know it is for you?"

"I don't know. The letters show up in random places, so I don't know if I should leave one in return somewhere. There's no guarantee that the right person would get it, you know?"

"Have you tried to figure out who it is?"

"Of course! But they're so random. One week I get two or three messages, the next one, then four. And they show up on different days, in different places. There's no way to spy and try to see who is leaving them."

"Hmm," I say as I ponder how to solve this mystery. "I can look out for it too. We should tell Maple and Olive too."

"Maybe," she says and I quirk a brow.

"You don't want to know?" I ask her and she shrugs.

"It's been nice. What if I hate the person who is leaving the notes? What if he's terrible and—"

"And the fantasy is ruined," I finish for her, and she nods. "I get it. Alright, I'll let you handle it."

"Thanks. Now, let's talk about you and your handyman."

"There's not much to say. He's working on the house, and we have our story figured out for when we see his family. A few more days and the deal is over."

"And how do you feel about that?" she asks me, and I sigh again.

"I don't know," I admit. "Scared? My feelings are already out of control for him, and I'm afraid that I'm going to get hurt when this is all over and done with. And then I have to live next door to him!"

"Tell him that it's not fake for you," she urges me.

"I'll look insane. Like a lovesick fool when I just agreed to fake dating him a few days ago."

"He likes you too."

"I can't risk it," I tell her, and she nods.

The bell over the door dings, and we both look up as a group of four older ladies come in. We both get to work, and I try to forget about Nolan and my growing feelings for him.

I don't succeed.

I know that this is only going to get worse. The more time that I spend with Nolan, the harder it is for me to separate what's fake and what's real.

As I close up for the night and start to head home, I realize one thing.

I'm in trouble, and I don't know how to stop from falling completely in love with Nolan. I'm not sure that I could stop it even if I wanted to. And that means one thing.

I'm screwed.

SIX

Nolan

"I'M NERVOUS. ARE YOU NERVOUS?" Saffron asks me as we pull up outside of my parent's place.

"I mean, now that you just told me that, yeah."

"You're not supposed to say that!" she scolds me. "You're supposed to tell me that I'm being silly and that everything is going to be fine, and they're going to love me and not to worry."

"Everything is going to be fine, and they're," I start to parrot back to her, and she scoffs and smacks my arm lightly.

Saffron has really started to warm up to me over the last few days. She's still quiet, but I can tell that she feels more comfortable in my presence, and that makes me unbelievably happy.

I laugh as I unbuckle and turn to her.

"Okay, for real, they're going to love you, and it's going

to be fine. We'll eat and then head home. It will be a piece of cake."

She takes a deep breath and nods, her fingers tightening around the pie that she brought for tonight. She still looks nervous, but it really is going to be fine. My mom is already half in love with her just based on the little information that I've already told her about Saffron.

"Let's do this."

We climb out of my truck and I frown up at the darkening sky. It's starting to snow, but it's light. As long as it stays that way, the roads should be good enough to drive back to Wolf Valley later.

My childhood home looks exactly as I remember it. I haven't been back in a while, not since I left for the Air Force. The house is a two-story ranch style, the outside decorated for fall with orange lights and pumpkins everywhere.

We head up to the front door, and I try to discreetly take a deep breath before I turn the knob and usher Saffron in ahead of me.

"Uncle Nolan!" Five little kids shriek as soon as I walk in the door.

"Hey, guys!" I greet my nieces and nephews.

They all start talking to me at once, and I smile as I crouch down and pull them into a tight hug one by one.

"Guys, this is my friend, Saffron. Saffron, these are my nieces and nephews. There's April, Andy, Ben, Samantha, and Troy."

They all stare up at her with big, curious eyes, and she smiles down at them.

"It's nice to meet you. Happy Thanksgiving," Saffron says sweetly.

"Nolan!" My mom yells as she barrels into the front room.

"Hey, ma. Happy Thanksgiving."

She beams at me as she wraps me up in a tight hug.

"My boy finally came home," she whispers, and I wince, feeling guilty that I've stayed away for so long.

I just didn't want to have to field all of my family's questions about why I was still single and how I was doing after leaving the military. I didn't want to talk about the accident or the aftermath. I couldn't answer their questions about what's next because I don't know what's next.

"And you must be Saffron!" My mom says as she turns to take in my girl.

"Hi, it's nice to meet you. I uh, I made a pie," Saffron says shyly, holding the pie out to my mom.

"You too, dear! Oh, it's so nice to meet you," my mom gushes. "Nolan hasn't told me much, so I'm so excited to get to know you better. Come and let me introduce you to everyone."

And just like that, I lose track of Saffron.

My mom drags Saffron around to meet all of my aunts and uncles. I try to keep track of her, but the house is so full that it's hard to get around.

"Hey, I met your girlfriend," my sister greets me, and I nod, scanning the room for a certain curvy redhead.

"Yeah? Where is she?"

"Kitchen. Surrounded by all of our aunts," Shelby tells me. "She's nice. How did you land her?"

"Luck," I grunt out, and she laughs.

"I believe it."

"Believe what?" Aaron, our youngest sibling, asks as he joins us in our corner of the living room.

"That Nolan lucked out with his new girlfriend," Shelby tells him.

"Oh yeah, she's great!" Aaron agrees. "My kids are already calling her Aunt Saffron. Or Aunt Saffy in the case of Samantha."

I laugh as I see Aaron's youngest clinging to Saffron's leg as she comes into the living room. Our eyes lock, and she smiles. She seems more at peace with my family than I feel, and a warm feeling starts to spread in my chest. I'm happy to see that everyone seems to love her right away, not that I can blame them. She's easy to love.

I'm the oldest of the three of us and the only one not married or settled down with kids yet. I'm also the only one who joined the military and left town.

"It's time to eat!" My Aunt Kathy calls, and everyone starts to head into the dining room and kitchen.

I find Saffron in the crowd and slip my hand into hers.

"Everything okay?" I whisper to her, and she nods.

"Everyone is so nice."

I squeeze her hand, and she leans into my arm a bit.

"Where are we sitting?" she asks me, and I look around.

"Aunt Saffy! Can you sit with me?" Samantha asks.

"You're at this table," Aaron tells his daughter as he leads her over to the kid's table in the kitchen.

Samantha pouts and Saffron looks upset.

"We'll sit close to their table," I whisper to her as I lead the way over to the far side of the adult's table.

"Hey, Nolan!" Mark, Shelby's husband, greets me. "How's it going?"

"Pretty good. How about you?" I ask him as I pull out a chair for Saffron.

We all sit down, and I turn to check in on Saffron. She's happy, busy talking to the kids at the table next to us.

"Your girl is lovely," My Aunt Sarah tells me, and I smile.

"How have you been?" I ask her.

We start to pass the food around the table, and I hold the bowl of mashed potatoes so that Saffron can grab some before I pass it to my sister-in-law.

"So, tell us how you two met!" My Aunt Kathy says, and I turn to Saffron.

"We're neighbors," she says with a small smile. "We met when I moved in next door to him."

"Are you from Wolf Valley?" My dad asks, and Saffron shakes her head.

"No, me and my sisters moved there about a year ago."

"Saffron opened up a bookstore in town," I tell my family.

"Oh, how exciting!" Aunt Kathy gushes.

The conversation focuses on Saffron, her bookstore, her family, her new house, and finally, our relationship.

"So, how long have you two been dating?" Shelby asks.

"A few weeks now," I tell them as I dig into the food.

We all dig in, and finally, the conversation changes to what everyone else has been up to. Everything seems to be going great. My mom and dad are thrilled that I'm with someone. Everyone seems to love Saffron, and it's great to see my family again.

Still, I can't help but be on guard. There's this nagging feeling in the back of my mind that keeps telling me that this is the end. Our deal is over after tonight, at least on her end. I'll just have to be around her all of the time as I fix her house, but I won't be able to hold her hand or pretend that we're together.

I try to focus on the meal, but every time that Saffron

laughs or looks at me with those soft eyes, I wonder if maybe it's possible to make this thing between us real.

Could it be possible that this isn't fake to her either?

SEVEN

Saffron

"THANK you so much for having me. Dinner was delicious and it was so nice to meet all of you," I tell Nolan's family as he holds my coat up for me to slip my arms into the sleeves.

"Oh, any time, dear!" Mrs. Wright tells me as she steps forward to wrap me up in a tight hug. "You're welcome back here anytime."

"Thanks," I whisper, and she smiles as she pulls back slightly.

"Thank you. It's nice to see my son so happy and I know that we have you to thank for that."

"I'll see you guys later," Nolan says as he hugs everyone good.

He takes my hand, and I smile, waving one more time as he pulls open the front door. I've liked getting to know his family, but I'm ready to head home and be alone to process all of my feelings.

Nolan pulls open the door, and a blast of snow and freezing cold air hits both of us, knocking me back a step.

"Whoa," I blurt out when I see how bad that weather has turned in the few hours that we were here.

A foot and a half of snow is now covering his truck, and more is still coming down.

"You can't drive home in that!" Mrs. Wright says, and I glance up at Nolan.

"Uh..." He says, blinking as he looks out at the weather.

"You'll stay the night. We insist. Right, honey?" Mrs. Wright says, nodding at her husband.

"Of course. I'll get the sheets for your old bed," he says, and I blink as he takes off down the hall.

"Nolan?"

"Um," he says, shutting the front door. "Maybe the snow will stop soon."

He pulls his phone out and we both frown when we see that it's supposed to snow for another few hours.

He looks at me, and I can see that he's nervous about my reaction.

"I...I guess we should stay."

"Yeah. We'll leave first thing in the morning," he assures me.

I nod and unzip my jacket. Mrs. Wright is clearly over the moon that we have to stay longer, and I smile at her as Nolan hangs my coat back up.

"Well, do you want to see my childhood bedroom?" he asks, and I can't help but smile at his obvious discomfort.

He looks so nervous, and now I'm curious about what it looks like. We were so busy all day that I didn't get a chance to tour the whole house.

He takes my hand and leads me down the hallway and into a bedroom. There are some old trophies on a shelf, some books, and a few trinkets. I smile as I walk around and look at all of it.

"Football?" I ask him as I look at the trophies.

"I wasn't very good," he says, and I smile.

"You have trophies so it kind of looks like you were," I point out.

"It was the team. Not me."

He's so modest and I kind of swoon as I move on to the little moose figurine.

"I made it when I was sixteen and went through my whittling phase," he explains, and I laugh.

"You make it sound like everyone has a whittling phase."

"Don't we?"

I turn to see him smiling at me, a twinkle in his eye, and my heart flutters in my chest so hard that, for a moment, I wonder if I'm having a heart attack.

My eyes stray to the full-size bed, and I swallow hard as I stare at it, knowing that soon, we'll both be sleeping in it.

"It's hard to imagine you fitting on that bed," I say, my voice coming out hoarse sounding.

"I didn't go through my growth spurt until I was eighteen."

I eye him, taking in his six-and-a-half-foot frame. My eyes trail over his muscles, and my mouth starts to water as I imagine his hard body pressed against mine.

"Saffron?" Nolan asks, and my eyes snap to his.

"Hmm?"

"Did you want to take a shower first? You can borrow some of my old clothes to sleep in."

"Sure."

He shows me to the ensuite bathroom and grabs me a

towel, some of his childhood sweatpants, and an old high school t-shirt.

"Your mom doesn't get rid of anything, huh?" I ask and he snorts.

"Nope. I haven't lived at home in years, and it still looks like it did when I was in high school."

"That's sweet," I say softly, and he smiles slightly.

"I'll let you take a shower. Let me know if you need anything else."

I nod, and he backs out of the bathroom, closing the door as he goes. I turn on the shower and try to ignore the way my body reacts as I use his body wash and shampoo. It's no use, though, and as I pull on his clothes, I'm more turned on than I've ever been in my life. My nipples are hard, poking against the thin material of his shirt. I fold my arms over my chest to try to hide them as I step back into the bedroom.

Nolan smiles as he stands and heads into the bathroom, and I try not to think about him naked and wet on the other side of the door. My core clenches and I start to grow wet as I listen to the shower running.

I press my thighs together to try to ease the ache as the water turns off. I try to act normally as the door opens and Nolan steps out, dressed in a pair of pajama pants just like mine, only his are a few inches too short.

I giggle, and he glares at me.

"Not a word."

"What? I think it's cute."

He tugs the pants down a bit, exposing an inch of his stomach, and my smile drops as I stare at that stretch of skin.

"I'll sleep on the floor," he tells me.

"Knock, knock!" His mom says, poking her head around

the door. "I brought some toothbrushes and toothpaste for you two."

"Thanks, mom."

"Thanks, Mrs. Wright."

"Of course. Do you two need anything else?"

"No, we're good."

"Okay, see you in the morning!"

"Night!" I call as she heads out, closing the door behind her as she goes.

Nolan passes me a toothbrush, and we head into the small bathroom. It's cramped as we stand shoulder-to-shoulder at the sink and brush our teeth. My eyes stray to him in the mirror and we both smile at each other, white toothbrush bubbles around our lips.

I spit and rinse my mouth out and then he does the same. He hits the light and we file back into the bedroom.

"You don't have to sleep on the floor," I tell him, and he turns to me.

"I don't mind."

"It won't be comfortable," I point out, and he shrugs.

"I want you to be comfortable."

"I'll be fine sharing with you."

He nods slowly, and I climb onto the bed. He hits the lights, and a moment later, the bed dips as he climbs in next to me.

"Good night," I whisper.

"Night, Saffron. Happy Thanksgiving."

"Happy Thanksgiving."

I close my eyes, trying to slow my racing heart as we lie in the dark next to each other. I can feel his heat, can hear his breathing next to me. I'm hyper-aware of him next to me in the dark.

I shift, trying to get comfortable, but it doesn't work.

Not when my body brushes against him, setting my whole body on fire.

"Saffron," he murmurs, and I can't take it anymore.

It's like I'm a bowstring being pulled tighter and tighter, and I'm ready to snap. I lean forward, my hands rubbing up his chest, and my heart races as I hear his sharp intake of breath. He tenses under my touch, and I lick my lips.

"Nolan." His name tastes like a promise on my tongue, and the intensity in his dark eyes makes my heart stumble in my chest.

He takes a step forward, just enough that I have to tilt my head back to hold his gaze. There's a charge between us, electric and unsteady, and it's pulling me closer, pulling both of us into something dangerous and delicious. I don't know who moves first, but suddenly we're right there, breathing the same air, so close I can feel the heat of him like a storm building.

His hand rises slowly, like he's giving me a chance to stop him. I don't. Instead, I lean into his touch, and when his fingers cup my jaw, I swear my bones melt under the warmth of his palm.

His warm breath fans my face, and we both pause, our eyes locking in the dim light from the moon outside.

"Saffron," he whispers, and my eyes flutter closed as his lips meet mine.

I instantly go up in flames. I press closer to him, until our bodies are tight against each other. I gasp as I feel his hard cock against my stomach. Part of me can't believe that he's turned on by me, but then my brain shuts off, and all I can do is get swept up in the passion between us.

We pull apart, both of us sucking in a breath. Our eyes lock, and my heart feels like it's going to beat out of my chest.

"Saffron," he whispers, like he's been holding my name in his mouth for too long, waiting for this exact moment to let it go.

I don't wait another second. I reach up, grab the front of his shirt, and yank him down to me. Our mouths collide in a kiss that's as wild as the storm outside, all heat and hunger and pent-up frustration. His lips are firm and demanding, and I match him, kiss for kiss, like I've been starved for him without even realizing it.

He groans low in his throat when I open my mouth under his, and the sound sends a thrill straight through me. His hand slides into my hair, tugging just enough to make me gasp, and he uses the moment to deepen the kiss, his tongue sweeping against mine in a way that makes my knees threaten to give out.

I clutch at his shoulders, desperate to stay anchored as everything inside me tilts, shifts, and catches fire. Nolan kisses me like he's trying to memorize every second, like he knows we've wasted too much time, and he's determined to make up for it now.

"Night, you two!" Nolan's dad calls through the door, and we jerk apart.

Nolan almost falls off the bed and I reach for him, both of us panting as we stare at each other.

"Night," I call back, my voice unsteady.

"Night, Dad," Nolan calls, sounding just as affected as I feel.

I clear my throat as I listen to his footsteps fade down the hall.

"We should get some sleep," I say, my voice hoarse, and he nods.

We settle under the covers, and I take a deep breath as I try to calm my racing heart enough so that I can fall asleep.

It takes a long, long time before sleep finally claims me.

EIGHT

Nolan

WHEN I WAKE up the next morning, Saffron is already out of bed. In fact, she's not even in the room anymore. Her clothes from yesterday are gone, and the pajamas that she wore to bed last night are folded on the dresser.

I sigh as I scrub my hands down my face and sit up in bed. My mind flashes back to that kiss last night. I'd never been cockblocked by my parents before since I never had a girlfriend before, and I do not recommend it. I had been so close to going all of the way with Saffron last night. I wanted to strip her naked, throw her legs over my shoulders, and eat her out until she screamed my name. Then I'd bury myself inside of her and make her scream my name all over again.

I guess it's a good thing that we didn't go all of the way. When I make love to Saffron, I want it to be romantic and not in my childhood bed, in my childhood bedroom, with my whole family sleeping right down the hall.

I get dressed and go to find my girl. She's in the kitchen, helping my mom make breakfast and laughing at something that Samantha is saying to her. My heart lodges in my throat, and I freeze as I stare at her.

She's perfect, and I want her. I want her so goddamn bad. I want her to be my real girlfriend, my real wife, the real center of my whole fucking world.

"Morning, honey!" My mom calls, and I blink, trying to clear the vision of Saffron in a wedding dress from my head.

"Morning," I rasp out.

Saffron blushes as she looks at me, and I know instantly that she's thinking about our kiss last night.

"How's the weather?" I ask.

"All clear! It's sunny and gorgeous out this morning," my mom says. "Well, besides the fact that it's about three degrees out."

Saffron laughs, and I smile as I move closer to her.

"Are you ready to head out?" I ask her, and my mom frowns.

"No way! You have to stay for breakfast."

I look at Saffron, and she nods.

"Alright. Let's eat," I relent.

As we sit down and start to eat, people are still waking up. Saffron and I both dig in, and we eat quickly. Samantha is talking Saffron's ears off, and I smile as I listen in on their conversation.

Once we finish eating, I clear our plates and go back to Saffron's side.

"Ready?" I ask her, and she nods.

I can tell that she's getting overstimulated from being around so many people. Saffron is like me and needs to recharge their social battery often.

"We're going to head out," I tell my mom and dad, and my mom pouts but nods.

"Thanks again for having me," Saffron says, stepping forward to hug my mom and then my dad goodbye.

"You're welcome anytime," my mom tells her, and my dad nods in agreement. "Oh! You have to come back for Christmas!"

"Yeah!" Samantha cheers, and Saffron smiles.

I can see the moment that she remembers our deal and that we won't be fake together by then. Her smile dims, and I swallow hard. My heart sinks because I want to spend every holiday with her and I'm not sure that's possible. Why did I make the deal for just one holiday? I should have said until the house was fixed and then dragged the projects out for years, until she was in love with me.

"Maybe," she says, and I nod.

"I'll talk to you guys later," I say as I step forward and hug my parents goodbye.

We make the rounds, saying goodbye to everyone, and then I help Saffron into her coat, and we head out to my truck. I help Saffron into the passenger seat and scrape off the windows while the truck heats up. Then we're hitting the road.

She's quiet as I maneuver us down the snowy streets.

"Everyone liked you," I say, trying to break the silence.

"Yeah, your family is great. The kids were so cute," she says, and I smile.

"Yeah, Samantha seemed to especially love you."

"She was so sweet."

"I'm glad that you had a good time."

"Me too," she says softly.

We drive in silence for a few minutes, and then she clears her throat.

"What excuse will you give them for Christmas?" she asks, and my stomach sinks.

"I... I don't know. I guess that you had plans with your family. It's the truth."

She nods, and we ride in silence for the rest of the way home. I was going to try to broach the subject of us together for real, but after her comment, I don't think that's a good idea.

I pull into my driveway and park, hurrying out to open her door for her and help her out.

"I can come over in a few to start on the house," I tell her and she blinks.

"You don't have to do that today. I'm sure that you have things to do."

"Nope, I'll be by in a bit."

She nods, and I watch as she walks over to her house and lets herself inside. I head into my own house and wonder what to do now as I close the door behind me and look at my empty place.

I change clothes and then grab my tools and head over to her house. I hesitate as I raise my hand to knock on the door and take a deep breath. I knock, and a second later, she pulls the door open and ushers me inside.

"It's freezing out! I was going to build a fire."

"I can do that," I offer, and she smiles.

"I should probably check first and make sure that it's safe to do it," she says with a laugh.

Her hair is damp, and she smells like strawberries and roses. I breathe deeply as I set my tools down and head over to the fireplace to see what we're working with. Surprisingly, the fireplace seems to be in great condition, and it takes me no time at all to start a fire.

"Thanks," she says, and I nod as I wipe my hands off on my jeans.

"What did you want me to start with first?" I ask her and she blinks as she stares at me.

I can't quite read her expression, not at first. We stare at each other, and she licks her lips, her green eyes darkening and filling with heat. My body reacts to that and I shift on my feet like a racer about to take off. My breath stalls in my lungs as I stare down at her.

I blink, and a second later, we're crashing together, the heat from last night flaring back to life between us as my lips move over hers.

She tastes like tea and honey, and I pull her closer against me. I don't want any space between us. Ever.

"You drive me crazy," I murmur, my voice low, like a confession wrapped in a promise.

My thumb strokes along her cheek, and I feel the pull between us. It's magnetic, inevitable.

"Nolan..." she whispers a second before our lips connect again.

The kiss deepens as her hands find the front of my shirt, curling into the fabric as if she needs something to anchor her. I tilt my head, deepening the kiss. My fingers tangle in her hair, and I tip her head back as I devour her.

The kiss turns urgent, like we're both afraid that the other will stop it before we're ready. Saffron melts into me, her lips molding to mine perfectly. My cock presses against her, and she moans as she rubs against it.

We break apart, both of us breathing hard. She stares up at me, her eyes a little wild and her hair coming loose from her ponytail. I love seeing her like this and knowing that I'm the only one who gets to muss her up and get her to lose control.

"Remember where my bedroom is from the tour?" she whispers against my mouth, and I grin.

"Uh-huh."

"Let's go."

I don't need to be told twice. I swoop her up into my arms and take off up the stairs and into her bedroom. She giggles, the sound like music to my ears as I lay her down on the bed and come down over her.

The bed is perfectly made and I grin, loving the idea that we're about to mess it up.

"I want you," she whispers, and I kiss her.

"I want you too. Fucking badly."

She smiles, seeming to grow more confident from my words, and her hands wrap around the back of my neck. She tugs me down, and our lips connect once again. She's so soft. All of her is soft, her lips, her skin, her curves.

Her hand tugs on my shirt, and I sit up, tugging it over my head and letting it drop to the floor. Saffron's eyes are on me, and I pause as she admires my chest. Her fingers tentatively run over my abs, and I'm thankful that I kept up with my workouts even after I left the military.

She licks her lips, and the restraint that I've been holding onto so tightly starts to fray.

"Need you. Naked. Now," I tell her and she tenses beneath me.

I frown. Did I read the signs wrong? I thought that she wanted me.

"We don't have to do anything that you don't want to, Saffron," I tell her, and she blushes.

"I want you," she says softly. "It's just...you look like that and I... don't."

Her blush heats her whole face, turning it almost as red as her hair.

"I love your body. I've been dreaming about these curves for so long," I tell her, my voice low and husky as I stare down at her body. "Can't you feel what you do to me?"

I press my erection against her, and her eyes go hazy with lust.

"I just... I've never done this before."

"Done what?" I ask, my brain still on the heated look in her eyes and how good she feels against me.

"Sex."

"Huh?"

That gets my attention, and I blink.

"How is that possible?" I ask her, and she looks away from me.

"Well, believe it or not, but guys weren't exactly lining up to sleep with the chubby bookworm."

"Why not?" I ask her, and she blinks.

"I...because...because I'm overweight and shy, and that's not what guys want."

"You're not overweight."

And that's exactly what this guy wants.

"I am."

"No," I argue.

"Like medically," she starts, and I press my hand over her mouth, cutting her off.

"I don't want to hear it. You're perfect. I don't like hearing you talk badly about yourself."

"Itsteemuf," she mumbles against my palm, and I shake my head.

"No. Perfect."

She rolls her eyes, but I can see the pleased look in their green depths. If she wants me to tell her how amazing I think she is, I can do that. I'll do that every damn day, all day long if she'll let me.

I can also show her.

"Perfect," I whisper again as I bow my head and kiss her neck.

She shivers and so I do it again.

"I love that you haven't been with anyone before," I whisper against her skin, and she frowns against my hand. "I'm a jealous bastard, and I wouldn't have been able to stand if there was another man out there who knew you that way."

My hand drops from her mouth as I reach for her shirt, and she arches against me, helping me pull it over her head. My eyes drop to her chest, and I groan.

"Fucking hell, Saffron."

She blushes, but I notice that the hands that were reaching to cover her have fallen back to the bed.

"God, I'm not going to last two seconds with you," I grumble as my lips hover over hers.

"Well, I guess that's one way to make my first time memorable," she says, and I snort.

She giggles, and I kiss her neck, trailing my lips down to her plump tits.

"Don't worry, baby. I'm going to make it memorable."

I'm going to make it so damn good for her that she never wants to sleep with anyone else. I'll make her fall just as hard for me as I have for her, and then we can be together. For real.

My hands cup her breasts, pushing them up until they start to spill over the cups of her bra. My mouth waters at the sight of her cherry-red nipples peeking over the edge of the satin cups, and I lick my lips as I lean forward and take one into my mouth.

"Oh!" she cries as my tongue rolls over the sensitive peek.

I reach under her, my fingers unhooking her bra, and I drag the straps down her arms and toss it to the side. My hands greedily cup her breasts, and I pinch one nipple between my fingers while I suck on the other one.

"Nolan!" she shouts, her hips writhing against mine.

My cock aches in my jeans, and I groan as she rubs against me. I need her, but I need to get her off first. Multiple times.

My hands release her tits, and I reach for her soft leggings, standing so that I can peel them off of her legs. Her white panties are next, and then she's laid out before me, completely naked.

I have to grit my teeth to stop from coming instantly. Her curves are perfect. She's so pale, with freckles scattered across her skin. I want to find each one and mark it with my hands and mouth.

My hands grip her thighs, and I pull her legs wide as I drop down to my knees at the edge of the bed.

"Nolan," she says, nerves clear in her voice.

"I'm going to make this good for you, Saf," I promise, and our eyes meet and lock.

She nods, and having her trust me means the world to me.

I push her thighs wider as my eyes lock on her pussy. She's already wet, and I almost come just from the sight of her arousal. She smells like honey as I lean forward and take my first lick up her center.

"Goddamn," I groan as her flavor bursts across my tongue.

"Nolan," she says, her voice shaky.

I glance up at her, checking to make sure that she's okay, and see her white-knuckling the comforter.

"More?" I ask, and she nods her head forcefully.

I grin and do as she says.

My thumbs spread her folds apart as I lean forward and bury my face between her legs. She cries out as my tongue licks over her clit, and I do it again and again, until she's trembling beneath me.

"Nolan!" she shouts as I suck her clit into my mouth, my tongue thrashing it, then rolling softly over that little pearl.

"Oh! Oh! Oh, my—" she cries, her thighs tensing on either side of my head.

I know that she's close, and I trail one thick finger down her core until I find her snug opening. My finger rims that tight hole, and Saffron's sucks in a deep breath, her whole body freezing as if she's balancing on the edge of a cliff. With one more flick of my tongue over her clit, she falls, and I'm right there to catch her.

"Nolan!" she screams, her voice ending on a sob as I push my finger into her slowly.

She's so tight, and I wiggle the digit slightly, trying to loosen her up a bit.

"Fuck!" she sobs, and I lick her clit lightly, drawing out her orgasm as I work my finger into her more.

"Nolan! Please," she sobs, and I look up at her body until our eyes meet.

I can feel her juices on my lips and chin, and she shivers as she stares down at me, her green eyes so dark.

"I want to try," she says, and I lick her clit again.

"Hmm?"

"I want to try to make you come," she says and I smirk.

"Saf, you keep looking at me like that and you're going to get your wish."

"I want to... use my mouth," she says, rising up on her elbows to look down at me.

I freeze, my finger still buried in her pussy, her juices coating my mouth and chin.

"I don't think that that's a good idea," I croak and she looks embarrassed.

"Oh."

"Shit, Saffron. You can suck me, baby, but hell, it's going to be embarrassing for me."

"Why?" She asks innocently.

"Because you're not even touching me, and I'm close to coming. You get anywhere near my cock, and I'm going to come so fast."

"I don't mind," she says, and I laugh.

She wiggles away from me, and my laugh cuts off. I frown, reaching for her hips to stop her, but she's faster.

She stands next to me, looking down at me, and I swallow hard.

"Why don't you let me fuck that pretty pussy a few times, and then you can suck my cock," I offer, and she shakes her head.

"Please, Nolan? Just for a minute."

I groan, pushing to my feet.

"You've gotta stop begging to suck my cock, Saf."

"You don't like it when I do that? You don't like dirty talk?" she asks, her voice dropping on the last two words.

She's so innocent. Fuck, I love her.

"I love it," I tell her, and she smiles.

"I can talk dirty," she says softly. "I've always been better with words."

I have no idea what to say back to that because I've never been good with words.

Saffron drops to her knees, and her hands reach for my jeans. She undoes the button, and I swear that I stop breathing as she tugs the zipper down and then pulls my jeans and boxers slowly down my legs.

I kick them to the side and close my eyes, taking a deep breath to try to control myself.

"You don't want to see me on my knees in front of you?" she asks breathlessly, and I screw my eyes shut.

"Fucking hell," I grumble, and then her hand wraps around my length, and my knees almost buckle.

"You're so big. I'm not sure that I'll be able to take all of you," she says, and I glance down at her, my mouth dropping open as I get my first look at Saffron kneeling before me, her little hand pumping my cock as she licks her lips and looks up at me.

She shuffles closer to me, her warm breath fanning over my sensitive skin, and I try to imagine hitting myself in the face with a hammer to stop from coming all over her pretty face.

"Saf," I start, but then she wraps those damn lips around my cock, and my mind blanks.

My breath comes out in a rush, and I almost drop to my knees as her tongue swirls around the tip. I catch myself on the headboard before I can crush her under me and suck in a sharp breath.

"Saffron," I say urgently, and she hums around my cock.

I see stars.

"Saf, baby, please."

She sucks so hard that her cheeks hollow out, and my eyes roll back in my head.

Fuck.

"Need you," I groan as I step away from her.

She blinks up at me, her lips wet and swollen, and I snap.

I reach down, scooping her up and dropping her in the

center of the bed. I crawl over her, kneeing her legs apart as I settle between them.

"Tell me that you're ready for me," I order, and she nods.

"I'm ready."

"Thank fuck," I grit out as my cock nudges against her opening.

We both tense as I start to push into her, and I grit my teeth as her wet heat surrounds me. I make it halfway inside of her and have to stop to regain my control.

"You feel so good," she moans, and I growl.

"Not helping."

"I want more."

"*Really* not helping," I stress.

"I want all of you," she says, her ankles coming up and locking around my waist.

"Fuck, Saffron."

"Exactly."

I thrust into her, giving both of us exactly what we need. She gasps, and I lean down, kissing her until her pussy stops trying to strangle my cock.

"I need you to move," she whispers against my lips, and I swallow hard as I do as she orders.

She feels so damn good, so hot and wet and tight. She really is perfect, and I want to tell her that, but all of my energy is being spent on not coming just yet.

"Oh! Oh my gosh, right there," she moans and I want to put my hand over her mouth again, but I'm using it to balance above her.

"God, I love your cock," she moans. "And your body."

Her hands run over my chest, her nails scraping lightly down my arms. She's driving me crazy. I've never been so turned on in my life.

"I never want you to stop fucking me," she tells me. "But I really want to feel you come in me."

"Fuck, Saffron!" I shout, and her hands grip my biceps, clinging to me as my pace starts to grow erratic and rough.

"Can I feel it?" she asks me innocently, and I curse under my breath. "I mean, you're fucking me raw so..."

She trails off, and I grit my teeth. She's right, though. I didn't even think about protection. I didn't want there to be anything between us, and I guess some part of me was hoping to knock her up and tie her to me forever.

"Saffron," I start, but I have no idea what I was going to say next.

"I want it. You wouldn't let me suck your cock and taste you that way, so coming in me is the least that you can do," she whispers, and I lean back on my heels, my cock pounding into her now.

"Please, Nolan?" she begs, and I nod.

My thumb finds her clit, and I rub it in times with my thrusts. She tightens around me, and I can tell that she's close. Two more thrusts, and she splinters apart around me, pulling me with her over the edge.

"Fuck!" I shout as I come deep inside of her.

"Oh! Nolan," she moans, her legs tightening around my hips.

I keep moving in her until I'm sure that her orgasm has passed. Then I promptly collapse on my side next to her.

"Whoa," she whispers, and I smile at her.

"Uh huh."

"Is it always like that?" she asks me sleepily, and I shake my head.

"No, or it never was for me. Although... I've only been with one person before. It was in high school, a decade ago, and it was quick and forgettable."

"What was her name?"

"I don't remember."

I can't remember any other girl but you, I want to say, but I'm worried that will come on too strong. After all, she still thinks that we were fake dating.

I need to fix that.

I catch my breath, and I know that I need to talk to her and tell her that this is real for me and that I don't want her to be my fake girlfriend. I need to tell her what she means to me.

I take a deep breath and turn to face her... only to realize that Saffron is fast asleep.

I try not to be too disappointed as I pull her into my arms and let my own eyes drift shut. As I drift to sleep, I vow to tell her that I love her tomorrow. Just as soon as I wake up.

NINE

Saffron

I TRY to get lost in books as I unpack the new boxes that came in, but my mind is still back in bed with Nolan.

This morning was anxiety-inducing. I wasn't sure if I should stay until he woke up and then I started thinking about his reaction to last night and getting freaked out that maybe he would wake up and regret sleeping with me. In the end, I panicked, got dressed, and bolted out of my house without waking him up.

It's been a few hours, and I haven't heard from him yet, which makes me even more concerned that he regrets our night together.

"Hey! How's it—Whoa! What's wrong?" Lilou asks, rushing over to my side.

"What?" I ask, blinking out of my spiraling panic.

"You look totally freaked out. What's wrong?" she asks as she tucks her purse behind the counter.

I take a deep breath and look around the shop before I lean closer to my friend.

"I slept with Nolan," I tell her.

"What!?" A voice shrieks by the front door, and my head snaps up, relaxing when I see my sisters, Maple and Olive, standing at the door.

"I, uh, I slept with Nolan last night," I tell them.

"You're fake boyfriend?" Maple asks at the same time that Olive says, "Your neighbor?"

"Yeah..."

"So, are you two officially together?" Lilou asks me.

"I... don't know," I admit. "We slept together, and then I left while he was still sleeping, and we haven't talked since."

"Well, do you want to be with him? Do you like him?" Maple asks me, and I swallow hard.

"Yeah, I do," I whisper.

"Then talk to him! Tell him that you want to really be his girlfriend," Olive tells me.

"I..." I trail off, and they all share a knowing look.

"It can be scary," Maple says gently, and I nod.

"What if he doesn't want to be with me? What if it was just a one-night stand for him or a mistake? Then I'll have to keep living next door to him and seeing him all of the time, and he's still fixing up my house, so that's going to make it even more awkward, and then I'll have to sell the house, and move to avoid him and—"

"Whoa! Slow down, Saffron. It's going to be okay," Olive says, her eyes wide with concern.

"You don't know that," I groan miserably.

"You need to talk to him," Lilou says, and I nod.

"I know, I'm just scared."

An image of Nolan above me, moving inside of me, fills my head, and I swallow hard. Last night felt so real, and I can't help but wonder if it just felt that way for me or if he felt it, too. Was it just a fling for him? Or something more?

"Just be brave and ask him. The worst that he can say is that it was just a one-time thing, and then you can work on moving on," Maple says.

"Hey! You guys all hanging out without us?" Ginger and Mira ask as they come into the bookstore.

"Saffron is freaking out, and we're helping her," Olive tells them, and I groan.

"Why?" Ginger asks.

"She slept with Nolan last night," Maple tells them.

"Woohoo!" Mira cheers, and I shake my head.

"I'm worried that it's just a one-night stand for him," I explain.

"It's not. I've seen him look at you, and he's always mooning over you," Mira says.

"Yeah! I mean, I wish that someone would look at me like that," Lilou agrees.

"Babe, I keep telling you that I'll look at you any way that you want me to," Milo says as he joins us in the store, and Lilou jumps, whirling around.

"We need to get a bell for the doors," she grumbles.

"How do you want me to look at you?" he asks her as he leans on the counter across from her. "Maybe like this? Over dinner?"

"No."

He just smiles at her, and her face flames bright red as she looks at anyone except him.

"Should we talk about Christmas? Is it too early for you to meet my parents?"

"Oh my god!" she shouts and throws her hands into the air.

His phone starts to ring and he smiles at Lilou before he answers it and heads back outside to his car.

"When is that going to happen?" Mira asks Lilou, and she glares at all of us when we giggle.

"Never."

"He's not going to give up," I point out. "He's been after you since he got to town. I haven't even seen him look at another girl."

"Never," she growls and we all know to drop it. At least for now.

"Now, when are you going to talk to your man?" Lilou asks me, and I sigh.

"I'll talk to him tonight," I tell them.

I even manage to sound confident as I say it, but deep down, I'm terrified that I might be the only one feeling this way.

I spend the rest of the day dreading when I have to go home and talk to Nolan. By the time I'm closing up Shelf Indulgence, I'm on edge and feel nauseous.

Time to get this over with.

TEN

Nolan

I WAKE UP ALONE, and it takes me a few moments
before I remember where I am and what happened yesterday. I smile as I remember everything that Saffron and I did
to each other last night. I sit up in bed and frown as I look
around. Saffron's side of the bed is cold, so I know that she
must have gotten up a while ago.

I toss the covers back and pull on my boxers as I go in
search of my girl. I can't help but wonder if it's a bad sign
that she wasn't still in bed with me as I make my way
through the house.

It takes me only a few minutes to realize that Saffron
isn't here. She must have gone to the bookstore already.

I frown as I stand alone in her half-remodeled kitchen
and wonder what to do now. I want to talk to Saffron about
last night and our future together, but I know her well
enough to know that she won't want to have that conversation at work.

So, I'll stay here. I'll work on the house and practice what I want to say to her when she comes home. Then we can have our talk and get on with our relationship. Our *real* relationship.

I've finished a lot of the bigger renovations around here already. The bathroom cabinets came in a few days ago so that room is done. The kitchen counters are on backorder so that will be a few more days, so instead, I get to work on a special project.

Saffron has a room off of the living room that she has no idea what to do with, but I know. It's going to be her home library. I've already sketched out the layout for the custom built-in bookshelves and a cozy reading nook.

I head into the room and start bringing in all of the supplies and cutting the boards to size. I'm going to leave the wood raw and let Saffron pick out all of the colors that she wants.

The repetitive task and the hum of the saw helps me clear my head and figure out what I want to say to Saffron when she gets home. I want to tell her that this was never fake for me and ask her to officially make this relationship real.

When my phone rings a few hours later, my heart lodges in my throat, and I hurry to answer it, hoping that it's Saffron calling to tell me that she's coming home early. Instead, it's my mom. I debate ignoring the call, but I know that she'll just call me again.

"Hey, mom."

"Nolan! I was just calling to make sure that you and Saffron made it home safely."

"Oh, yeah, sorry, I should have let you know."

"No worries. I know that you two were probably busy. We loved meeting her by the way! She sure is a keeper."

"She sure is," I agree.

"Are you going to bring her back for Christmas?"

"Um, I'm not sure. I think that she might be celebrating it with her sisters."

"Oh, well, you two could come down before or after too! We'd love to see you both again. Oh! Or maybe for New Year's!"

"Maybe," I tell her noncommittally. "I'll have to ask Saffron."

Right after I ask her to be my girlfriend for real.

"Okay, well let me know. I'll let you go and talk to you later."

"Sounds good. Talk to you soon, mom."

"Love you."

"Love you too."

I hang up, and a minute later, I hear Saffron's car pull into the driveway. My heart takes off like a shot, and I head out of the library to greet her at the door.

I take a deep breath as she walks up the front porch steps, and as soon as she walks inside, I open my mouth and blurt out, "We need to talk."

ELEVEN

Saffron

THINGS AREN'T OFF to a great start.

I planned on out everything when I left work. I would walk into my house and find Nolan, then try to figure out how he was feeling about last night and how awkward things were before I asked him if we could talk.

Instead, he beat me to the punch.

"Uhh," I start, my hand still on the doorknob.

"About last night," he says, trying to comfort me.

Really, it has the opposite effect.

We stare at each other for a beat and then I close the door and peel off my coat and hang it up.

"Okay."

He swallows, and we head into the kitchen, each of us standing on either side of the counter as we stare at each other.

"How was work?" he asks, and I blink.

"Good. How about you?"

"Good. I have a surprise for you."

"Really?"

"Yeah, but first, I wanted to talk to you about last night and about...us."

"Okay," I whisper.

"I..." he closes his mouth, and I watch him swallow hard once more. "I love you."

"What!" I gasp, my mouth dropping open.

"I love you, Saffron. I have for months, well before I asked you to be my fake girlfriend for Thanksgiving. God, I never should have done that. I never want anything between us to be fake."

My knees feel weak, and for a second, it feels like I'm in the middle of one of my romance books.

"You regret it?" I ask him and he frowns.

"No, not really. I can't ever regret any time that I spent with you."

I grin, and he seems to relax.

"You love me?" I ask him softly, and he nods.

"So much, Saffron. So damn much. I should have just talked to you. I should have asked you out weeks ago, I should have told you about how I felt from the beginning, definitely before we slept together."

"I kind of panicked this morning. I should have stayed and talked to you and told you how I was feeling," I tell him, stepping closer to the kitchen island.

He nods, a hopeful look in his dark blue eyes.

"I love you too, Nolan. I've had a crush on you since I moved to town and first saw you, but I never thought that you would be interested in me. I didn't think that you noticed me at all," I admit.

"You were all that I noticed," he tells me, and I smile as a blush spreads across my cheeks.

"So, last night..."

"Was everything that I dreamed it would be and more," he finishes.

"Yeah, it was."

We share a smile, and he takes a step towards me.

"So, we're doing this? We're together? Officially?" I ask, and he nods.

"Fuck yes. You're my girl, Saffron. For real."

"For real," I agree.

We close the distance between us, and he wraps his arms around my waist, pulling me flush against him. My hands cup his face and he smiles down at me as his lips slowly lower to claim mine.

His lips move against mine slowly, like he's cherishing me, like he has all of the time in the world to kiss me. I moan as I lean against him, loving the feel of his strong body against mine.

"Mine," he whispers, and I nod.

Nolan's lips mold to mine and I get swept away by his kiss, by the feel of his hands on my back, pulling me closer and closer still.

When he finally pulls back, I feel like I'm floating, drugged by his kisses. His hands rub up and down my back, like he can't stop touching me, and I smile up at him.

"Do I get my surprise now?" I ask him, and he grins.

"Yeah, come on."

He takes my hand and to my surprise, leads me down the hallway to the bedroom off of the living room. I'm not sure what I was expecting, but it wasn't a wall of bookcases. If I wasn't in love with him before, seeing this would have had me falling head over heels for him.

"Oh my gosh! It's perfect!" I gush as I rush over to run my fingers over the wooden shelves.

"I didn't paint or stain them yet. I thought that you might want to pick out the colors and stuff."

"I love it! Thank you so much!"

"Of course," he says, smiling as I run over to him and wrap him up in a tight hug.

It doesn't take long for both of our bodies to react. It's like we can't be in the same room with each other now without needing to rip each other's clothes off.

"I need you," I whisper, and he nods.

His hands grab my hips, and he pulls me into him. I can feel his dick starting to swell against my thigh, and I can't help but rub against it. I feel wanton and desired as his cock hardens even more. I shift so that the thick ridge is between my legs, right where I need him most, and I can't help but moan. It feels so good, so hard.

"Fuck, Saffron," he groans, and I smile shyly up at him.

Nolan's head dips, his warm breath hitting my face, and my eyelids flutter shut as his lips land on mine. My heart is racing, and as my hands rub up his chest, I can feel that his heart is beating out of control, too.

My fingers climb higher, and I run my hands over his collarbone, memorizing every line of his body as I go. Nolan backs me up a step, and I go willingly. My fingers trace along his jawline, and he pulls away, staring down at me. I trace around his ear, my fingers tangling in his dark locks, toying with the long strands. I want to run my hands over all of him, to trace his body, and map it in my brain.

"I really love you," he murmurs, and I grin.

"I really love you too."

His lips capture mine as his hands move up my ribcage until he's cupping my breasts in his big, capable hands. His hands knead the soft globes, and I break the kiss, pulling away as I moan, my head falling back.

Nolan kisses down my neck, his lips finding the pulse point at the base of my throat. I push into him, wanting his hands on my skin, on every inch of me.

I raise my hands over my head, letting him drag the thin cotton of my shirt over my head. He wastes no time and drags the cup of my bra down next, exposing my nipples to the cold air. They pucker instantly, tightening into stiff peaks.

"Fuck, you're so perfect, Saffron," Nolan whispers against my heated skin, and I gasp as his warm mouth sucks the tight bud into his mouth.

His tongue swirls around it, and I arch into him. My eyes flutter open, and I watch as the fan spins round and round on the ceiling above us. Nolan's hands go around my back, and he pulls me into him, his hands tangling in my purple hair as he devours my breasts.

I swear that I'm about to explode. My whole body feels like it's on fire. I'm hot and needy, aching for him to make me come.

Everything about Nolan turns me on. The toned abs, the full lips, and dark blue eyes, the chiseled lines of him, all of the dips and planes. All of it is a work of art that I want to admire for hours. He's so strong, so smart and capable. He's sexy and funny, but right now, it's his body that is doing it for me.

Nolan pulls back, and I bite back a needy whine, missing having his mouth on me.

"Bed. Now," he orders, and I nod.

We take off up the stairs and into my bedroom. I giggle as we seem to race for my room, and as soon as I'm there, I'm pushing down my pants as I back up toward the mattress.

Nolan's eyes are burning, glinting in the sun as he takes

me in and I straighten my shoulders, wanting him to look his fill. It's obvious that my body turns him on just as much as he turns me on.

Nolan pushes me down onto the bed, and I start to wiggle out of my panties, letting Nolan pull them the rest of the way off.

"Fuck. Every inch of you is a dream, Saffron."

My body warms at the compliment, and I hold my hand out to him, wanting to feel his weight on top of me. He pulls his shirt off first, kicking his shoes off as he pushes his pants down his toned legs.

He comes down over me, and I spread my legs. He's still wearing his boxers, so we're not skin-on-skin, but I can still feel how hard and hot he is.

His head dips again, and his mouth latches onto one of my nipples, sucking the whole thing into his mouth. His mouth is so hot and wet, the suction so perfect that I'm close to coming in seconds.

My toes curl into the sheets as my hips rock restlessly against his, and he switches to my other breast.

That spot between my legs is getting wet, tiny sparks going off with every bite, suck, and caress that he gives my breasts. It's not quite enough, though. The nagging emptiness between my legs just won't go away, and the dull ache is starting to drive me crazy with need. I need to do something. I need him. I push on his chest, and he lets my nipple go with a pop, leaning up to look at me questioningly.

"I want to take care of you," I say, my fingers running down his chest, following his happy trail down to the band of his boxers.

Nolan pushes off of the bed, reaching for his boxers, and I drop to my knees, helping him pull them down his legs.

They pool at his feet, and he steps out of them as I reach up, fisting his thick length.

I open my mouth wide, sucking in the tip of his cock as Nolan's hand tangles in my hair. He doesn't push on my head, he just rests his hands there, his fingers tugging on the strands as my head starts to bob.

The feeling lights up my scalp, and I moan as I take more of him into my mouth. I work my hand in time with my mouth, and my body only burns hotter as I feel him swell against my tongue, hear the moans and the way that he says my name like it's a prayer.

"Fuck," Nolan says, pulling me off of him, and he reaches down, dragging me up to my feet and then pushing me onto the bed.

I pull him down, and our lips meet; we cling together as we take our time exploring each other. The earlier rush is gone, and I moan, rolling him onto his back and straddling his hips.

"Let me lick your pussy," Nolan says, but I shake my head.

I'm already wet enough, and I know that if I let him do that, he'll take control again, and I want to set the pace this time.

I reach behind me, grabbing his dick and lining it up with my opening as I slowly sink down, taking him into my body inch by delicious inch.

"Fuck," he hisses out as I slowly sink down until he's fully seated inside of me. "You're so wet. So fucking hot."

I grin at him, resting my hands on his chest as I slowly roll my hips. We both moan with every rock of my hips, every in and out, every push and pull of his cock inside of my snug channel.

His hands go to my ass, groping the globes, using them

to pull me down harder onto him. I pant as I grind against him, and he leans up, sucking one of my tits into his mouth.

He takes over, thrusting up from beneath me as our mouths fuse together, and I can feel myself starting to splinter apart around him as the pressure inside of me builds.

He hits a certain spot deep inside of me, and that's all it takes to send me flying over the edge of the cliff into oblivion.

Nolan's brow furrows in concentration as he grips my hips and drives into me in perfect precision.

Seeing him like that is intoxicating, and I can't look away as he finds his own release inside of me.

He rolls us to our sides, and we both suck in a deep breath as he pulls me against his chest.

"Love you, Saffy," he says, making me laugh.

"Love you too," I tell him as I drape my arms around his shoulders.

I feel his lips brush against my forehead, and I smile as I cuddle into his side.

"I'm going to need to do that again," he tells me, and I grin.

"Uh huh," I agree.

"But first, I should probably feed you."

"Just when I thought that you couldn't get any more perfect," I joke, and he grins. "My own knight in shining armor."

"I'll be anything that you need, Saffron," he whispers against my lips, and I smile.

"The food can wait," I whisper back, and he grins as I press my hips against him in invitation.

"Whatever you want, Saffy."

And he proceeds to give me everything that I want.
All. Night. Long.

TWELVE

Nolan

FIVE YEARS LATER...

I CARRY OUR THREE-YEAR-OLD SON, Finn, on one hip as I balance a casserole dish with my other hand. Finn is busy babbling about the dinosaurs he saw in his picture book this morning, completely oblivious to the fact that I'm breaking a sweat trying not to drop him or the sweet potato casserole I promised Saffron's sisters I'd bring.

"Daddy, I'm a T-Rex!" Finn announces proudly, lifting his arms and giving a tiny, ferocious roar.

"Yeah, buddy. You're the scariest one," I reply, grinning despite the precarious juggling act I'm managing.

Behind me, Saffron is closing the car door, holding our six-month-old daughter, Ellie, against her chest. Ellie's in that perfect stage where she's still soft and sleepy most of the time, and her big green eyes—the same ones Saffron has —blink up at me with curiosity.

"Need help?" Saffron asks, arching a brow as I readjust Finn for the third time.

"I've got it," I lie.

Saffron laughs softly, knowing better. She steps closer, brushing her shoulder against mine as she smiles. Even after all these years, she still manages to steal my breath every time she looks at me like that, like I'm the only person in the room.

"Ready for the chaos?" she teases, giving me a knowing grin.

"Is anyone ever really ready for Baker-family chaos?" I shoot back, pressing a quick kiss to her temple.

She snickers, and together, we head up the walkway to Olive's house. The front door is already cracked open, and we can hear the laughter and noise pouring out from inside.

The moment we step through the door, the usual Thanksgiving madness unfolds. Olive is directing traffic, shouting instructions about platters and pies from the kitchen. Ginger and Ryder are already in the thick of a lively debate with Townes and Mira about something to do with the parade floats on TV, and Kip is chasing his twin daughters around the living room, narrowly avoiding disaster as they shriek with laughter.

"Uncle Nolan!" one of them yells the second she spots me.

Before I know it, Finn's squirming out of my grip, eager to join the chaos. He takes off toward the twins without a second glance back, roaring like a dinosaur the whole way.

"Bye, buddy," I call after him, though he's already gone, wrapped up in the whirlwind of his cousins.

Olive swoops in before we can catch a breath. "Finally!

The dream team is here." She beams at Saffron and me, then takes the casserole dish from my hand. "You two are late, by the way."

"Blame the kids," I say, nodding toward Finn, who's now wrestling on the floor with Kip's girls.

"Excuses, excuses." Olive grins and winks at Saffron. "Glad you survived the morning, though. I know what it's like."

Saffron snorts, adjusting Ellie in her arms. "Barely. But hey, we're here."

We settle in quickly, the flow of conversation and noise wrapping around us like a familiar, chaotic blanket. Xavier waves me over to where he's stationed with Fisher and Huxley, beers in hand, already immersed in the sacred Thanksgiving tradition of sports talk. I grab a drink and join them, feeling more relaxed than I did years ago at my first Baker Thanksgiving.

It's not just familiarity—it's the comfort that comes with knowing you belong. This group, with all their quirks and teasing, is my family now. And Saffron? She's everything good in my life wrapped up in one perfect, chaotic package.

At some point, I catch sight of her across the room, Ellie now asleep against her shoulder. Saffron's laughing at something Olive said, her face lighting up in that way I can never get enough of.

We've had our fair share of hard days, raising two kids isn't exactly a walk in the park, but moments like this remind me how lucky I am. Watching her, surrounded by the people who love her, I feel like the luckiest man alive.

We moved into the house after I had finished fixing it up and I sold my old one. We got married there at the house, in a small ceremony in the backyard with just our friends and families there in attendance.

I started my own remodeling business a few years ago, and it's really taken off. I've hired a few guys to work for me and that gives me ample time to spend with my family or helping Saffron out at the bookstore. I even volunteer as the classroom monitor at the kid's preschool every Monday.

Since our wedding, we've taken turns switching between who's family we spend holidays with. It doesn't make the holidays any less chaotic, but Saffron says that it's the only fair way to split things up.

She catches me staring and gives me a soft, knowing smile. I smile back, my heart feeling so full I can hardly stand it.

"Time to eat!" Olive calls, and I tear my gaze away from my wife to find my Finn.

Dinner is, predictably, a mess in the best way. Kip's twins start an impromptu food fight over the mashed potatoes, which Finn is all too eager to join. Saffron scolds him, but I can see the smile she's trying to hide.

"Boys," she mutters, shaking her head. "They get it from you, you know."

"Not sure what you mean." I grin, wiping mashed potatoes off Finn's nose and earning a giggle from him.

Once the food is demolished and everyone's too stuffed to move, Olive pulls out a stack of games. It's tradition now. Thanksgiving isn't complete without a little friendly competition.

"Alright," Olive announces, holding up the cards for couples' trivia. "Let's see if the reigning champions can defend their title."

I groan dramatically. "You mean the reigning cheaters?"

Ginger gasps in mock offense. "Excuse me, we *never* cheat."

Saffron laughs beside me, nudging my arm. "We're

winning this year," she says, her eyes sparkling with mischief.

"You think so?" I ask, wrapping an arm around her shoulders and pulling her close.

"I know so."

The game goes about as well as expected, with plenty of trash-talking and not-so-subtle hints that certain couples are "totally peeking" at the answers. Saffron and I do better than I thought we would—five years together has given us an edge, even if we do bicker over which of us snores more (it's totally her, but I let it slide).

When the final question rolls around: "What's one thing your partner does that drives you crazy?"—I don't even have to think.

"She talks to her plants," I say with a grin, earning an uproar of laughter from the room.

Saffron just rolls her eyes, clearly used to this one by now. "They need encouragement," she says matter-of-factly, earning even more laughter.

"And I wouldn't change it for anything," I add quietly, just for her.

She looks up at me, her eyes soft, and smiles in that way that makes my heart feel like it's going to burst right out of my chest.

Later, when the kids are asleep in the guest room, and the house has finally quieted down, Saffron and I step out onto the porch to catch a moment of peace. The stars are bright above us, the air crisp and cold. I pull her close, wrapping an arm around her shoulders, and she leans into me, her head resting against my chest.

"You good?" I ask, pressing a kiss to her hair.

"Mmm. Better than good," she murmurs, her voice soft and content.

I hold her a little tighter, letting the quiet settle around us.

"Thanks for everything," she says after a while, her voice barely above a whisper.

I smile, brushing a strand of hair from her face. "You don't have to thank me, Saffron."

She tilts her head back to look up at me, her eyes shining in the moonlight. "I know. But I want to."

And just like that, I know I'd do it all over again—every chaotic holiday, every sleepless night, every crazy, beautiful moment we've built together.

Because with her?

This life is exactly where I want to be.

WANT MORE OF SAFFRON AND NOLAN? CHECK OUT THIS BONUS SCENE OF THEIR FIRST CHRISTMAS TOGETHER!

WANT A FREE BOOK?

You can grab Sweets **Here.**
**Check out my website, www.shawhart.com for
more free books!**

ABOUT THE AUTHOR

CONNECT WITH ME!

If you enjoyed this story, please consider leaving a review on Amazon or any other reader site or blog that you like. Don't forget to recommend it to your other reader friends.

If you want to chat with me, please consider joining my VIP list or connecting with me on one of my Social Media platforms. I love talking with each of my readers. Links below!

Website
Newsletter

A Very Mountain Man New Year

Folklore

Kidnapping His Forever

Claiming His Forever

Finding His Forever

Rescuing His Forever

Chasing His Forever

Folklore: The Complete Series

Holiday Hearts

Be Mine

Falling in Love

Holly Jolly Holidays

Love Notes

Signing Off With Love

Care Package Love

Wrong Number, Right Love

Kings Gym

Fighting Fire With Fire

Fighting Tooth and Nail

Fighting Back From Hell

Mine To

Mine to Love

Mine to Protect

Mine to Cherish

<u>Mine to Keep</u>

Mine to: The Complete Series

<u>Sequoia: Stud Farm</u>

Branded

Bucked

Roped

Spurred

<u>Sequoia: Fast Love Racing</u>

Jump Start

Pit Stop

Home Stretch

<u>Telltale Heart</u>

<u>Bought and Paid For</u>

<u>His Miracle</u>

<u>Pretty Girl</u>

<u>Telltale Hearts Boxset</u>

Still in the mood for Christmas books?

Stuffing Her Stocking, Mistletoe Kisses, Snowed in For Christmas, Coming Down Her Chimney

Love holiday books? Check out these!

For Better or Worse, Riding His Broomstick, Thankful for His FAKE Girlfriend, His New Year Resolution, Hop Stuff, Taming Her Beast, Hungry For Dash, His Firework

Looking for some OTT love stories?

Her Scottish Savior, Baby Mama, Tempted By My Roommate, Blame It On The Rum, Wild Ride, Always

Looking for a celebrity love story?

Bedroom Eyes, Seducing Archer, Finding Their Rhythm

In the mood for some young love books?

Study Dates, His Forever, My Girl

Some other books by Shaw:

The Billionaire's Bet, Her Guardian Angel, Falling Again, Stealing Her, Dreamboat, Making Her His, Trouble